THE DARK SIDE

Witches

and Warlocks

illustrated by David West
and
written by Anita Ganeri

PowerKiDS
press™

New York

Published in 2011 by The Rosen Publishing Group, Inc.
29 East 21st Street, New York, NY 10010

Designed and produced by
David West Books

Designer: Gary Jeffrey
Editor: Ronne Randall
U.S. Editor: Kara Murray
Illustrator: David West

Picture credits: 12bl, Marshall Astor; 13b, Hans Hillewaert; 15r, Huwmanbeing; 20tr, Kareesa Tofa; 20bl, antmoose; 20br, lrargerich21t, Dominik Schwarz; 21br, Bartholomew Dean; 24b, Bundesarchiv;

Library of Congress Cataloging-in-Publication Data

West, David, 1956-
Witches and warlocks / illustrated by David West and written by Anita Ganeri.
p. cm. — (The dark side)
Includes bibliographical references (p.   ) index.
ISBN 978-1-61531-901-5 (library binding) — ISBN 978-1-4488-1574-6 (pbk.) — ISBN 978-1-4488-1575-3 (6-pack)
1. Witches—Juvenile literature. 2. Warlocks—Juvenile literature. I. Ganeri, Anita, 1961- II. Title.
BF1566.W464 2011
133.4'3—dc22
                                              2010002776

Manufactured in China

CPSIA Compliance Information: Batch #DS0102PK: For Further Information contact Rosen Publishing, New York, New York at 1-800-237-9932

Contents

Introduction

Many bizarre creatures roam the world of mythology. Their origins may be lost in the mists of history, but they have preyed on people's superstitions and imaginations since ancient times. They include witches and warlocks, practitioners of magic and sorcery. For millennia, people all over the world have believed in witchcraft, perhaps as a way of explaining mysterious events or misfortunes. But are all witches and warlocks evil? Or can a witch's supernatural powers also be used for good? In modern times, witches and warlocks have become popular in movies, fiction, and fairy tales. Are you ready to go over to the dark side. It will send shivers down your spine . . .

Witches

An ugly old woman, with long, bony fingers reaching into the air, chants a mysterious verse to summon up the supernatural powers of the dark side. This is the popular image of the witch!

The witches that we find in books, movies, and TV shows represent just one idea of what a witch is like. This idea mostly comes from European beliefs. Witches that appear in myths from other places are very different creatures. Despite their reputation, witches are not always bad. Some use their witchcraft for good rather than evil. They are known as white witches, rather than black witches.

The Pythia could be thought of as a witch. She was the priestess of the Delphic Oracle, through which the Greek god Apollo spoke.

Witches are often shown as crones.

A white witch can heal damage caused by a black witch.

Recognizing a Witch

According to various myths and folklore, witches could be recognized by particular marks on their bodies, the tools of their trade, and the animals they kept.

During the witch hunts of the sixteenth and seventeenth centuries (see page 16), witches were said to have a mark on their skin, known as the witches' mark or Devil's mark. It was permanent and made by the Devil's claw or his branding iron when the witch made a pact with him. The mark was always in a hidden place, such as under the armpits or eyelids.

A broomstick was said to be a witch's wand in disguise, giving the witch the power of flight. A witch's broomstick was also known as a besom.

In old drawings and paintings, witches are often seen with a huge cooking pot, known as a cauldron, heating on an open fire. Inside there were the ingredients of magic potions or ointments—usually plants believed to possess supernatural powers. Mixing a potion while chanting a verse was one way to summon up the powers of evil spirits.

This woodcut picture (inset) shows witches raising a hailstorm. A witch (left) draws a magic circle to protect herself while mixing a potion in her cauldron.

This drawing depicts a witch feeding her familiars—two toads and a cat.

In folklore, a black cat is often associated with witchcraft and superstition (as a bringer of bad luck). It is probably the most common witches' familiar.

In witchcraft folklore, witches often kept animals, which were known as familiars. Black cats, bats, frogs, toads, ravens, and spiders were popular familiars. They would help a witch carry out her magic—helping her perform spells, sometimes acting as magic spies, and warning of danger.

Witches in Europe

The first witches we know about in Europe feature in Greek and Roman mythology. In pagan times, witches were respected for guarding people against evil spirits. They only became linked with the Devil when Christianity spread through Europe.

Two witches of ancient Greek myths were Hecate and Circe. Hecate was the goddess of witchcraft. She was usually shown with three heads (one dog's, one snake's, and one horse's) or in triplicate. Circe was the daughter of Helios, god of the Sun. In Homer's *Odyssey*, Circe turned Odysseus's men into pigs when they landed on her island, Aeaea.

A triple statue of Hecate.

In Greek mythology, Circe was said to cast her spells with magic potions.

Medea was another witch of Greek mythology. She was the granddaughter of Helios and a follower of Circe and Hecate. She used her magic to help the Greek hero Jason on his mission to find the Golden Fleece. Later, she married Jason and restored Jason's father to youth using her magical powers.

Medea mixes her magic potions to protect Jason from danger as he searches for the Golden Fleece.

England's most famous witches were the Lancashire witches, or Pendle witches. In 1612, 13 men and women were tried as witches and accused of the murders of 17 people. They were said to have sold their souls to evil spirits in return for magical powers and killed their victims by making and breaking clay pictures of them. Four of the so-called witches actually confessed, and ten were hanged, even though there was no evidence against them.

A Pendle witch imagined by an artist

Baba Yaga is a witch from Slavic folklore. In Russian folktales, she carries children away on her broomstick and flying mortar. Her house is supported by dancing chicken legs. This shape may have come from the shape of storage houses of the time.

11

Witches Around the World

Witches appear in the myths and folklore of cultures all over the world. Some peoples still believe in witches and witchcraft and in shamans and medicine men who battle the dark side of witchcraft.

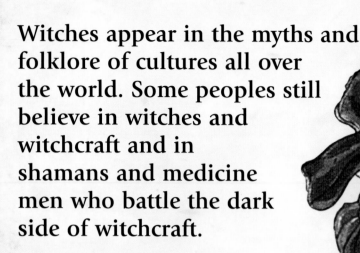

The *Kitsune-mochi* and Rangda are examples of witches from Asia. "*Kitsune*" is the Japanese word for fox. Japanese witches, called *Kitsune-mochi*, have fox familiars that are famous for their cunning and trickery. Rangda is queen of the witches on the island of Bali. She is the leader of a witch army that fights the powers of good.

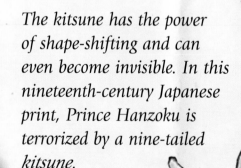

The kitsune has the power of shape-shifting and can even become invisible. In this nineteenth-century Japanese print, Prince Hanzoku is terrorized by a nine-tailed kitsune.

Rangda appears as an ugly old woman with long hair, claws, and often a long tongue. She is a popular figure in traditional Balinese dancing.

Some shamans beat a drum to send themselves into a trance. Other props include a headdress, a staff, and a rattle.

The word "shaman" means "one who knows." Shamans are believed to be links to the spirit world. People chosen as shamans can communicate with the dead, heal the sick, and see into the future. But some shamans can also be wicked. Shaman beliefs are found in Asia, Africa, North America, and Australia.

In southern Africa, a medicine man (who can be a man or a woman) is similar to a shaman. Known as *sangomas*, these medicine men are said to heal the sick (who are often thought to be bewitched), and so release people from witches' spells. They use traditional materials, such as stones, plants, and sticks.

Many African tribes have their own medicine men. Because sickness is sometimes thought to be caused by witchcraft, medicine men were once also called witch doctors, but they are not witches.

Spells and Curses

Witches make their magic happen with spells or charms that they cast on people or objects. A spell sparks the power of spirits either good or evil.

Witches weave their spells by carrying out rituals. Different rituals are used to create spells for different purposes. In the popular view of witchcraft, witches create spells with incantations (chants) and by mixing potions. Other rituals involve wax or clay dolls (called poppets) that are images of people. When the doll is harmed, the person is harmed, too.

A witch brews a potion for a spell in her cauldron. She can also see the future or faraway events in the water in the cauldron.

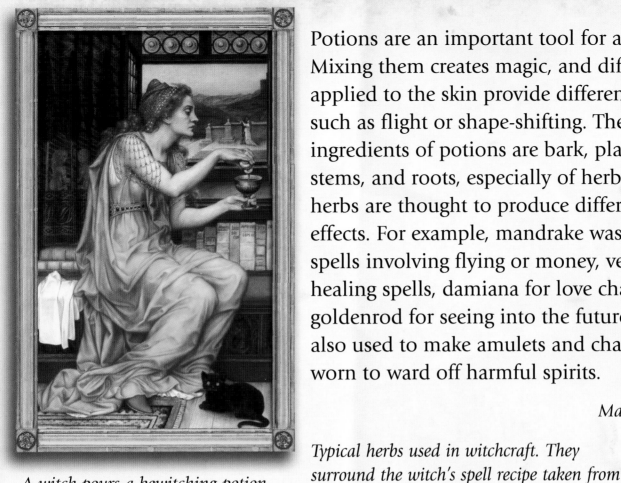

Potions are an important tool for a witch. Mixing them creates magic, and different potions applied to the skin provide different powers, such as flight or shape-shifting. The main ingredients of potions are bark, plant leaves, stems, and roots, especially of herbs. Different herbs are thought to produce different magic effects. For example, mandrake was used for spells involving flying or money, vervain for healing spells, damiana for love charms, and goldenrod for seeing into the future. Herbs are also used to make amulets and charms that are worn to ward off harmful spirits.

A witch pours a bewitching potion into a victim's drink.

Typical herbs used in witchcraft. They surround the witch's spell recipe taken from the play Macbeth, *written by William Shakespeare around 1600.*

Mandrake

Damiana

Goldenrod

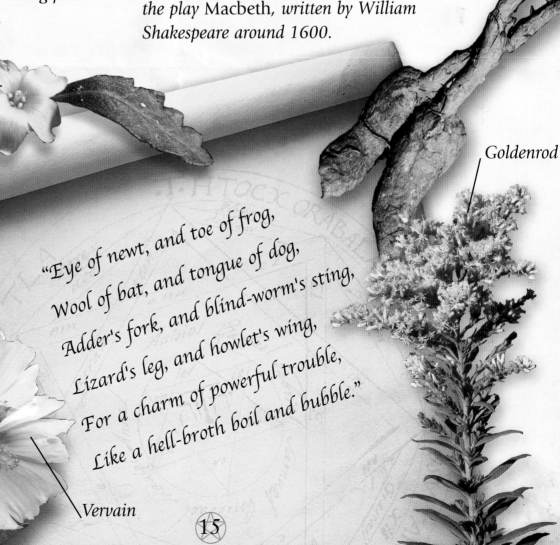

"Eye of newt, and toe of frog,
Wool of bat, and tongue of dog,
Adder's fork, and blind-worm's sting,
Lizard's leg, and howlet's wing,
For a charm of powerful trouble,
Like a hell-broth boil and bubble."

Vervain

Witch Hunts

In fourteenth-century Europe, a climate of fear and suspicion began to surround witchcraft. Encouraged by church leaders, who preached that witches were Devil worshippers, witch hunters mercilessly hunted down suspects.

Witch hunts reached their height between the 1580s and the 1670s. Even a whispered rumor could lead to a person being arrested. Suspects were tried using peculiar methods, such as pricking their skin to see if they felt pain and searching for a Devil's mark (see page 8). In some countries, suspects were tortured until they confessed.

Unfortunate men and women found guilty of witchcraft were burned at the stake or hanged. In all, about 50,000 people were executed.

A witch finder oversees a "swimming." Suspects were ducked into water. If they didn't drown, it supposedly proved they were guilty.

A special court was set up in Salem to try the witchcraft suspects. This nineteenth-century painting imagines the trial of one of the witches.

This painting depicts the arrest of a suspected witch in Salem. She is shown as an old hag—the common image of a witch. Most Salem "witches" were falsely accused for reasons such as family rivalry.

The fear of witches spread to European colonies around the world, including America. One of the most famous witch trials took place in 1692 in the town of Salem in the Massachusetts Bay Colony. Some young townswomen claimed that they had become possessed by the Devil. They accused other women of having bewitched them. Rumors and antiwitch hysteria spread through Salem. There was no real evidence of witchcraft, but 150 men and women were arrested. Eventually 19 were found guilty at the Salem witch trials and hanged.

Hags and Banshees

The popular picture of a witch is of a fearsomely ugly old woman or hag. This image may have come from the hags that appear in folklore from the British Isles.

A hag (or crone) is the name used mainly in Britain and North America for an ugly, evil-looking, old woman with wizened skin. Hags are often linked to witchcraft and other magic. They were supposed to create nightmares by sitting on the chests of their victims. Among the hags of British folklore are the terrifying Black Annis and the Scottish cailleachan, or storm hags. They are blamed for creating stormy weather.

Black Annis, or Black Agnes, is a blue-faced crone with iron claws who is said to live in a cave in the English county of Leicestershire. She emerges at night to hunt children and livestock.

Yuma-uba is a spirit monster from Japanese folklore. She takes the form of an old hag with long, untidy hair and dirty, torn clothes. She lives in the mountains and changes her appearance to trick and catch her victims.

Irish and Scottish folklore feature the banshee, or *bean sidhe*, which means "woman of the fairy mounds." She is a female spirit and the omen of death. In myths, she appears when someone is about to die, making a screeching mourning call. The banshee normally appears as a hag, with the frightening face of an ugly, old, long-haired woman, dressed in white or gray. Sometimes she is seen washing the blood-stained clothes of people who are about to die.

Because the banshee makes a moaning sound as she mourns the dead, she is often known as a wailing banshee.

Modern-Day Witches

People in many countries around the world still believe that witches exist and that witchcraft can do both good and evil. There are even modern religions based on witchcraft.

Wicca (the old English word for witch) is the name of a modern-day witchcraft movement in Europe and the United States. Followers of Wicca call themselves witches and say that Wicca is their religion. Wiccan ideas are based on witchcraft traditions that were practiced in northern and western Europe before Christianity spread there. Stregheria is a similar Italian witchcraft-based religion.

Wiccan rituals often take place inside a magic circle (above) that is supposed to create a magic space.

Wiccan priestesses (below) perform special rituals.

Wiccans also worship the Greco-Roman goddess Selene.

There is a widespread belief in witchcraft among African, Asian, and Native North American and South American tribes. Some African tribes think that people are born witches and carry the powers of witchcraft in their stomachs. These so-called witches are blamed for illnesses and other bad luck. Sadly, people are occasionally killed if they are suspected of witchcraft.

In the west African religion of voodoo, sorcerers and sorceresses called botono claim to be able to call upon evil voodoo spirits. These spirits can bring misfortune or harm to their enemies.

Tribes from many countries have witchcraft traditions that go back for hundreds or even thousands of years. They have witchlike shamans (see page 13) who are said to use the power of the spirits to heal illnesses and tell fortunes.

A Kapsiki crab sorcerer from Cameroon. He claims to be able to predict the future by studying the movements of a crab in a pot.

An Urarina shaman from Peru

Warlocks

Standing in the center of a magic circle is a robed figure with flowing hair, a long beard, and a staff. He is a warlock, and he is calling on the spirits for the power to do his work.

A warlock is the male version of a witch. "Wizard" is another word for a warlock. Warlocks are also sometimes called magicians and shamans. Sorcerers and necromancers are similar. There are many famous warlocks in myths and legends as well as in stories and plays. Like witches, warlocks have the power to do good and evil.

Druids were the priests and judges of the ancient Celts, who lived in pagan times, over 1,500 years ago. They may have been the basis for the myths of warlocks.

Odin was the chief god in Norse myths. He was associated with magic and prophesying. In this image, he has the appearance of a warlock, with long hair, a hat, and a staff.

Warlocks and Wizards

The word "warlock" means "a person who breaks oaths or deceives." Some warlocks are said to receive supernatural powers at birth. Others learn to be warlocks by studying and learning from other warlocks.

Warlocks perform the same tasks as witches. They cast spells to control events (such as shape-shifting), help or harm people, see into the future, and talk to the dead. They use magic plants, incantations, and props such as crystal balls, wands, and staves. Alchemy is a dark art related to wizardry. Alchemists attempted to make gold from ordinary metals, such as lead and copper. They also tried to find cures for diseases and to discover the secret of immortality.

A warlock summoning the spirits of the dead

Alchemists attempted to make a substance they called the philosopher's stone by mixing materials and summoning the spirits. This substance was supposed to turn metals into gold.

24

The soothsayer Calchas predicted how long the siege of the Greek city Troy would last. He also advised that Agamemnon's daughter Iphigenia be sacrificed to the goddess Artemis so that the winds would blow Agamemnon's ships to Troy.

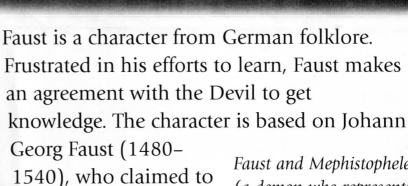

A seer, or soothsayer, is a warlock who has the ability to see people, objects, and events in the future or from a distance. The most famous seer in history was the French physician and astrologer Nostradamus (1503–1566). He wrote rhymes that predicted the future and became famous when some of his predictions appeared to come true.

Faust is a character from German folklore. Frustrated in his efforts to learn, Faust makes an agreement with the Devil to get knowledge. The character is based on Johann Georg Faust (1480–1540), who claimed to be an alchemist, astrologer, and magician.

Faust watching a magic disk, in a 1650 painting by the artist Rembrandt

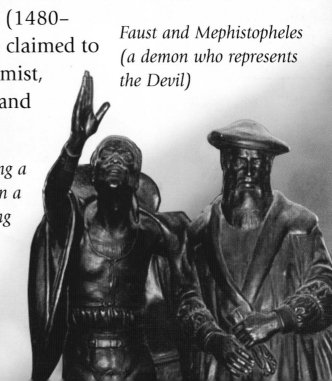

Faust and Mephistopheles (a demon who represents the Devil)

Sorcerers and Necromancers

In medieval folklore, a sorcerer was a warlock or wizard who practiced malevolent magic, or magic meant to do harm. A necromancer is a warlock who communicates with dead people, also for harmful purposes.

Sorcerers are also different from warlocks because they have to learn magic techniques. Warlocks often have supernatural powers within them. Sorcerers are feared by people because of their connection with frightening spirits, including the Devil, and because they use poisons in their spells. However, in ancient times and in popular culture, a sorcerer could do good as well as bad. Sorcerers often wear objects called pentacles around their necks. These objects have patterns on them, such as a five-pointed star within a circle, which are thought to give them power.

A sorcerer and the demon spirits he has summoned

Necromancers often visited graveyards because they thought that freshly buried corpses still contained some energy they could use in their spells. They even used parts of the dead bodies in their rituals.

The word "necromancy" comes from the Greek words for "dead" and "prophecy." A necromancer believed that the spirits of the dead could predict the future or perform a task for him. Necromancy, as a form of black witchcraft and black magic, was popular in European myths from medieval times. It was also practiced in ancient times, thousands of years ago, in the civilizations of Egypt, Greece, and Rome.

A grimoire (pronounced GRIM-wahr) was a handbook of magic written in medieval Europe. It was like a magic cookbook, containing spells, potion recipes, and magic symbols.

Famous Warlocks

A few real-life warlocks are well-known names in the world of witchcraft. Other warlock names have become famous because they feature in books and movies.

Perhaps the earliest warlock was Hermes Trismegistus. He was the Greek god of astrology and alchemy and may also have been a real person who lived many thousands of years ago. He was the author of parts of *Hermetica*, which were ancient writings on astrology, the spirit world, and alchemy. John Dee (1527–1608) studied the *Hermetica*. He was an alchemist, astrologer, and adviser to Elizabeth I of England, and spent years trying to contact angels. He dabbled in the supernatural with another alchemist, Edward Kelley.

Hermes Trismegistus, author of an ancient guide to the dark side

John Dee and Edward Kelley raising a spirit

Edward Kelley

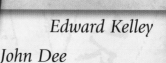

John Dee

In Arthurian legend and other Celtic mythology, Merlin is a warlock or sorcerer. His name first appears in the twelfth-century *History of Kings of Britain*, by Geoffrey of Monmouth, where he is adviser, prophet, and magician to Uther, Arthur's father. More recent famous warlocks are Gandalf, from J.R.R. Tolkien's works and Dumbledore, from the Harry Potter stories, by J.K. Rowling. Prospero is a magician in Shakespeare's play *The Tempest*. He uses magic to raise a tempest (a terrible storm) but later decides to give up magic for good.

According to legend, Merlin takes Arthur to a lake where the Lady of the Lake gives Arthur his famous sword, Excalibur. Later, Merlin is imprisoned forever by the Lady of the Lake.

In The Tempest, *the magician Prospero controls Ariel, a sprite. He makes Ariel perform magical tasks.*

Glossary

branding iron (BRAND-ing EYE-urn) An iron heated for making a mark on an animal's skin.

crones (KROHNZ) Witchlike old women.

folklore (FOHK-lawr) The traditional stories and legends of a particular place or people.

hysteria (his-TER-ee-uh) A state in which people's emotions run out of control.

immortality (ih-mor-TAH-lih-tee) Living forever; never dying.

medieval (mee-DEE-vul) Relating to the Middle Ages, a period of European history from around the fifth to the fifteenth century AD.

mortar (MOR-tur) A bowl-shaped pot, used for grinding herbs and spices.

myths (MITHS) Traditional stories, not based in historical fact but using supernatural characters to explain human behavior and natural events.

pact (PAKT) An agreement between two sides.

pagan (PAY-gun) In ancient times, people who did not believe in one God.

predictions (prih-DIK-shunz) Statements telling the future.

prophesying (PRO-feh-sy-ing) Telling the future.

rituals (RIH-choo-ulz) Set ceremonies or procedures.

shape-shifting (SHAYP-shift-ing) The power to change form from human to animal, animal to animal, or animal to human.

Slavic (SLAH-vik) Related to Russia and the countries of eastern Europe.

supernatural (soo-per-NA-chuh-rul) Magic powers and beings, such as fairies and ghosts.

trance (TRANTS) A sleeplike state.

witchcraft (WICH-kraft) The use of magic powers.

Further Reading

Allen, Judy. *Fantasy Encyclopedia*. New York: Kingfisher, 2005.

Ganeri, Anita. *An Illustrated Guide to Mythical Creatures*. New York: Hammond, 2009.

Guiley, Rosemary Ellen. *Witches and Wiccans. Mysteries, Legends, and Unexplained Phenomena*. New York: Checkmark Books, 2009.

Hamilton, John. *Witches. World of Horror*. Edina, MN: ABDO & Daughters, 2007.

Hill, Douglas. *Witches and Magic-Makers, 2nd ed.* New York: Dorling Kindersley Limited, 2000.

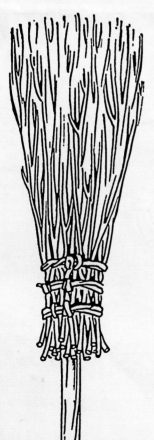

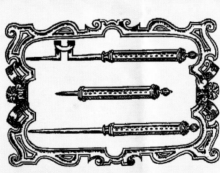

Witch-pricking needles

Matthew Hopkins, an English witch-hunter who accused many of witchcraft from 1645 to 1646

A besom

Baba Yaga rides a pig.

Index

A
alchemy, 24

B
Baba Yaga, 11
banshees, 18, 19
branding iron, 8

C
Calchas, 25
Circe, 10
crones, 7

D
Dee, John 28
Druids, 23
Dumbledore, 29

E
familiars, 9
Faust, 25
folklore, 8, 9, 12,
 18, 19, 25, 26

G
Gandalf, 29
grimoires, 27

H
hags, 18, 19

Hecate, 10
Hermes Trismegistus,
 28
hysteria, 17

I
immortality, 24
incantations, 14, 24

K
Kelley, John Edward, 28
kitsune, 12

L
Lancashire witches, 11

M
Medea, 10
medicine men, 12, 13
Merlin, 29

N
necromancers, 23, 26, 27
Nostradamus, 25

O
Odin, 23

P
pentacles, 26

philosopher's stone, 24
poppets, 14
potions, 14, 15
Prospero, 29
Pythia, 7

R
Rangda, 12

S
Salem witch trials, 17
Seers, 25
shamans, 12, 13, 21
shape-shifting, 12, 15
sorcerers, 21, 23, 26, 27
spells, 9, 14, 15, 24, 26
Stregheria, 20

V
voodoo, 21

W
warlocks, 23, 24, 25, 28, 29
Wicca, 20
witches' mark, 8
witch finders, 16
witch hunts, 8, 16, 17
wizards, 23, 24, 25

Web Sites

Due to the changing nature of Internet links, PowerKids Press has developed an online list of Web sites related to the subject of this book. This site is updated regularly. Please use this link to access the list:
www.powerkidslinks.com/darkside/witches/